DATE DUE			
MAR 2 9 2003			
APR 2 2 2008			
AUG 2 2 2011			
OCT 2 6 2013			
GAYLORD			PRINTED IN U.S.A.

Tales from the Story Hat

TALES FROM
THE STORY HAT

by Verna Aardema

Illustrated by Elton Fax

Introduction by Augusta Baker
STORYTELLING AND GROUP WORK SPECIALIST
THE NEW YORK PUBLIC LIBRARY

Coward-McCann   New York

To Paula and Charles Jon, to the Africans who gave us the tales, to the pupils of Lincoln School who helped me to tell them, and to story-loving boys and girls everywhere.

Fourth Impression

© 1960 by Coward-McCann, Inc.

Library of Congress Catalog Card Number: 60-6852

MANUFACTURED IN THE UNITED STATES OF AMERICA

CONTENTS

Introduction   7
Tricksy Rabbit   9
Wikki, The Weaver   18
The Sloogeh Dog and the Stolen Aroma   24
Madame Giraffe   32
Monkeys in the Sausage Tree   38
Nansii and the Eagle   44
How Dog Outwitted Leopard   49
Koi and the Kola Nuts   54
The Prince Who Wanted the Moon   62
Notes on the Stories   67
Bibliography   69
Glossary   70

There is a storyteller in West Africa who wears a story hat. It is a wide-brimmed hat of guinea corn straw and from its brim dangle many tiny carvings done in wood and ivory. Bits of fur, tips of feathers, and a leopard tooth intersperse the carvings.

Whoever asks for a story picks an object — and the storyteller is off on whatever tale it represents.

Stories in this book are akin to those he tells — he who carries his stories in his head and the Table of Contents on his hat.

INTRODUCTION

Today the eyes of the world are upon changing Africa. Modern civilization is forcing the ancient civilization of this great continent into the background. Large buildings are appearing in hitherto small towns, modern transportation is being introduced, and educated young Africans are going to work in efficiently organized offices. Yet, these eager, alert people will never give up all of their old traditions. This early civilization had its own high level of culture. For generations and generations there have been tribal laws which enforced rules of behavior. Their stories show that honesty and goodness have been rewarded while dishonesty and treachery have been justly punished. Ancient Africa had its poets, musicians, dancers and artists, skilled craftsmen and artisans as well as farmers and warriors — and, above all, it had its storytellers.

Storytelling, in Africa, has always held a place of importance and esteem. Most Africans have a large repertoire of stories which they enjoy sharing. The old women of the tribes have told these stories to the children just as grandmothers have done all over the world. There have been professional storytellers who have gone from place to place telling their tales and gathering new ones. They were the first historians and the first literary members of the tribe, and it was they who preserved and handed down traditions.

A great deal can be learned about a people from their folk tales.

Primitive man used the story to interpret the natural, spiritual, and moral world in which he moved. These stories became a part of the rich cultural and social heritage of the African. They show the philosophy, wisdom, and wit of the people and their wonderful sense of humor. They tell about men who are clever as well as stupid, who are good as well as bad. Their stories explain the African customs and mores, as in "Wikki the Weaver," where the art of weaving is developed. The origin of animals is often told, and in "The Prince Who Wanted the Moon," monkeys, gorillas, and baboons come from man rather than man from monkeys. There are many trickster type stories, and the main heroes of these tales are Hare and Anansi. "Tricksy Rabbit" and "Nansii and the Eagle" are good examples of these stories which are wise as well as very humorous. Rabbit became the United States' Br'er Rabbit, and Anansi or Nansii became the West Indies' Br'er Anansi. Many folklorists have felt that the African tales, with their high degree of sophistication and formalism, are true art forms.

As in other folklore, many African stories are not suitable for children, but the ones in this collection are neither too subtle nor too complicated, so that they will be easily understood and appreciated by young readers. The storyteller will add them to his repertoire because they tell well. This book is the result of the author's life-long interest in Africa and her study and research on the subject. Elton Fax has just returned to the United States from Africa where he was on an assignment as artist-reporter for the *New York Age*. These drawings, which catch the spirit of the stories, have come out of this experience.

Augusta Baker
Storytelling and Group
Work Specialist
The New York Public Library

8

Tricksy Rabbit

In Uganda, deep in the heart of Africa, there once lived a clever rabbit. He was so full of fun and tricks that the forest folk called him Tricksy Rabbit.

On the trail one day Tricksy met his friend Elephant. The two stopped to chat. "I hear," said Tricksy, "that the Watusi herders are in need of cloth. I would like to get a fine fat cow for myself. This may be a wise time to go trading."

"That is a fine idea!" said Elephant.

So the two prepared bales of cloth for the journey. Tricksy gathered a rabbit-sized bundle, and Elephant an elephant-sized one.

They set out for the land of the Watusi in a gay mood. Tricksy told one funny story after another. He kept Elephant squealing with laughter.

Presently they came to a river.

Elephant, who loved the water, waded right in.

9

"Wait!" cried Tricksy. "You aren't going to cross without me, I hope! Aren't we partners?"

"Of course we're partners," said Elephant. "But I didn't promise to carry you and your pack. Step in! The water is hardly over my feet."

"Over your feet is over my head," cried Tricksy. "And you know I can't swim!"

"I can't help that," said Elephant. "If you can't take care of yourself on the trail, then go back home." And he splashed on across the river.

"I'll get even with him for that!" muttered Tricksy as he set about looking for a small log. He found one nearby and, placing his bundle on it, paddled across the river. He paddled so fast to catch up with Elephant that he splashed muddy water all over the cloth. Though he wiped off the mud the best he could, the cloth was ruined.

Tricksy soon overtook Elephant, and the two reached the land of the Watusi with no more trouble.

Elephant went straight to the men of the tribe and told them he had come to trade his cloth for cattle. He was so gruff about it that at first the tall proud herders refused to deal with him. At last they agreed to give him a knobby-kneed little calf for his fine bale of cloth.

Tricksy went among the women. He laughed and joked with them and told them how pretty they were. They liked him so much that when the subject of trade was brought up, the wife of the chief was happy to give him the finest cow in the herd for his muddy little bundle of cloth.

As the traders set out for home, Elephant said, "Now if we should meet any strangers, you tell them that both animals belong to me. If anyone were to guess that such a fine cow belonged to a rabbit, it would be as good as gone. You would never be able to defend it!"

"You're right!" said Tricksy. "I'm glad you thought of that."

10

They hadn't gone far when they met some people coming home from the market. The strangers gathered around the cows to look them over.

"How beautiful the big one is," one man said.

"How fat!" said another.

"How sleek!" said a third.

Then a man approached Elephant. "The big cow is yours, I suppose. And does the little one belong to your small friend?" he asked.

Elephant coughed and tossed his head, preparing to boast that both belonged to him.

But Tricksy was too quick for him. "Ha!" he cried. "The *big* one is mine! Elephant and I went trading. I traded a small bundle of cloth for this fine cow. But all Elephant could get for his big bundle of cloth was that scabby little calf!"

The people had a good laugh over that!

The two went on. When they had gone a little way, Elephant said, "Tricksy, you shamed me in front of all those people! Next time let me do the talking."

"Those weren't the kind of people who would steal my cow anyway," said Tricksy.

Soon they met more people. They, too, stopped to look at the cattle. One man said, "That sleek fat cow couldn't be the mother of that rat-eaten calf, could she?"

Elephant opened his mouth to explain, but again Tricksy was too quick for him.

"No, no relation!" cried Tricksy. "You see, Elephant and I have been trading with the Watusi. And I, for a small bundle of muddy old cloth — "

He never finished, for Elephant swung his trunk and sent him rolling.

11

The people scattered in a hurry.

Elephant said, "A fine partner you are! You can't keep a promise from here to a bend in the road. Take that cow of yours and go home by yourself!"

So, at the first branching of the path, Rabbit separated from Elephant. From then on he knew he would never get his cow home safely unless he used his wits. He started to think.

Elephant hadn't gone far when he met a lion. "I happen to know," he told Lion, "that there's a rabbit with a bigger cow than this over on the next trail."

Soon he met a leopard, and then a hyena. He told them both the same thing. "One of the three will relieve him of that cow, for sure!" he chuckled.

Over on the next trail, the lion soon overtook Tricksy. "Rabbit!" he roared. "I could eat you in one bite! But go away fast — and I'll be satisfied with the cow!"

"Oh, Bwana Lion," cried Tricksy, "I'm sorry, but this cow isn't mine to give! She belongs to the Great Mugassa, the spirit of the forest. I'm only driving her for him to his feast. And, now I remember, Mugassa told me to invite you if I saw you!"

"Come now," said Lion, "are you trying to tell me that Mugassa has invited me to a feast?"

"Are you not the king of beasts?" asked Tricksy. "Surely he must plan to honor you! Anyway, come along and see!"

Lion fell into line behind Tricksy and the cow. They hadn't gone far when the leopard overtook them.

Leopard sidled up to Lion and said in a big whisper, "How about sharing the cow with me? You can *have* the rabbit!"

Tricksy overheard what Leopard said, and he broke in. "Bwana Leopard, you don't understand! This cow doesn't belong to either Lion or me. It belongs to Mugassa. We're just driving it to the feast for him. And, now I remember, I was told to invite you, too!"

"I'm invited, too," said Lion. "Mugassa is planning to honor me."

"Hmmm!" said Leopard. But he followed along behind the cow, the rabbit, and the lion.

Soon the hyena joined the procession in the same way.

13

A little farther on, a huge buffalo blocked the path. "Out of my way!" he bellowed.

"Oh, Bwana Buffalo," cried Tricksy, "I'm so glad you happened

14

along! We're taking this cow to the feast of Mugassa, and I was told to invite you. I didn't know where to look for you. Now, here you are!"

"Are all of you going?" asked Buffalo.

"Yes," said Lion. "Mugassa is planning to honor *me*. Perhaps I shall be crowned!"

"Hmmm!" said Leopard.

Buffalo turned around and led the procession with Tricksy riding on his head to direct him.

Soon they arrived at Tricksy's compound. Two dogs who guarded the gate yapped wildly when they saw them. Tricksy quieted the dogs and sent one streaking off to his hut in the middle of the wide compound with a pretend message for Mugassa.

In a short time the dog came back with a pretend answer, which he whispered into Tricksy's ear.

Tricksy stood on a stump and spoke importantly. "Mugassa says that hyena is to butcher and cook the cow. Lion will carry water for the kettle. Buffalo will chop wood for the fire. Leopard will go to the banana grove yonder and watch for leaves to fall. We need fresh leaves for plates.

"Dogs will lay out mats inside the fence. Then, when the meat is cooked, all of us must help carry it in and spread it on the mats. When all is ready, Mugassa will come out and present each his portion.

"One warning — Mugassa says that if anyone steals so much as a bite, all of us will be punished!"

Tricksy gave Lion a pail with a hole in the bottom. He gave Buffalo an ax with a loose head. He told Leopard to catch the leaves with his eyelashes so as to keep them very clean. Then he climbed to the top of an anthill to watch and laugh.

The animals were so anxious to hurry the feast that Tricksy had many a chuckle over their foolish efforts.

Lion hurried back and forth from the river to the kettle with the leaky pail. Though he filled it to the top each time he dipped it into the river, there would be only a little water to pour into the kettle.

16

Every time Buffalo swung the ax he had to hunt for the head of it, for it always flew off into the bushes. At last he finished breaking up the wood with his feet.

Leopard fluttered his eyelashes at the long banana leaves, but not one came down.

Now, Hyena had never before in his life had a choice of meat. Always he had to eat what was left by other animals. This time he saw and smelled the choice parts. The liver smelled best to him. "I hope Mugassa gives me the liver!" he said. "But he won't. He'll think the rack of bones to clean is good enough for me — me, who did most of the work!"

Hyena lifted the liver out of the pot and hid it under a bush.

Tricksy saw him, but said nothing.

When the meat was done, all the animals helped carry it in and spread it on the mats laid out in Rabbit's compound. Then Tricksy began to check. "Four legs," he said, "back, sides, neck, tongue. . . . But where's the liver?"

Everyone began looking for the liver. "Someone has stolen the liver!" cried Tricksy.

"Here comes Mugassa!" cried one of the dogs. "Run! Run!"

The big animals stampeded through the gate. Tricksy slipped the bolt through the latch. Then he and his dogs rolled on the grass with laughter.

They were still laughing when Elephant poked his head over the gate. "I see you got home, Rabbit!" he called.

"Yes!" said Tricksy. "I got my cow home, too — and all cooked already!"

"What I should like to know," said Elephant, "is *how* you did it."

"With the help of Mugassa," laughed Tricksy.

17

Wikki, The Weaver

In West Africa there once lived a hunter named Wikki. He brought so much meat into his village that he was made chief. But his name is remembered above the names of many hunters and chiefs, for it was Wikki who first learned how to make cloth.

Wikki's head wife, Salifu, and his bad wife, Umpo, helped. Umpo didn't know she was helping. She was just being her wicked self.

Umpo was envious of Wikki. When she would hear anyone boast of his skill as a hunter, she would say, "Huh! He's not so clever! He just has a strong ju-ju!"

Wikki would have been the last person in the world to question the power of his ju-ju. He made it himself — a fresh one each time just before he set out to hunt. And he told no one the secret of what went into his ju-ju bag.

Now, each evening when Umpo saw Wikki preparing to hunt, she would watch. And when he went into his hut to make his ju-ju, she would go into her hut and make a charm against it. She wanted to small him down a little.

But then in the morning Wikki would come home from the hunt with another buffalo. And Umpo would know that her charm was not as strong as his.

One evening when Umpo saw Wikki go into his hut to make ju-ju, she peeked through a crack in the wall. She saw him take a small bag made from the skin of a poisonous spider. Into it he put three hairs from the tail of the last buffalo he had killed, three small shavings from its horn, and a drop of black liquid from a jar. He tucked the small bag into his armlet, picked up his spear, and set out.

When Wikki was out of sight, Umpo crept into the hut. By the light of his fire she found another spiderskin bag. Into it she put three hairs from the tail of the last buffalo he had killed, three shavings from its horn, and a drop of black liquid from the jar.

She tucked the small bag into her armlet and whispered, "Destroy the power of Wikki's ju-ju. Let him hunt with his own strength alone!" Then she said to herself, "Now we shall see if he is as great a hunter as everyone thinks!"

Wikki went to the valley where the buffalo grazed. He heard them tramping and stamping and snorting as they fed. He was careful to stay down-wind from the herd. And he waited until the moon rose and spread a soft gray light over the grassland.

Then he picked a good fat bull at the edge of the herd, crept as close as he dared, and threw his spear.

But the spear only wounded the bull. With a bellow he charged. He caught Wikki on his horns and threw him into a thicket.

Wikki was lucky to escape with his life. He came crawling home the next morning with a badly hurt leg.

Umpo hadn't thought about harm coming to Wikki with the defeat of his ju-ju. When she saw how badly he was hurt, she feared she would be punished. She fled from the village and was never heard of again.

Wikki could not hunt for a long time. But he spent much time in the valley where the buffalo came at night to graze. He would sit on a log and think of battles he would have with the great beasts when he could hunt again.

One day, as Wikki sat dreaming at the edge of the plain, he saw a big black beetle fly into a spiderweb. The beetle kicked and fought the web until it was caught fast. Then the spider, who had been hiding, came out and began to eat it.

"You pass me, Spider," said Wikki. "You make the net fight for you. If I hunted that way I would not have a hurt leg."

Wikki decided to make a net. He went into the forest and cut a heap of bush rope. Then he set to work, crisscrossing the ropes and tying them here and there. By evening he had made a big net.

When Salifu saw the net, she was amazed. She called all the other wives to see what Wikki had made to hunt for him.

Wikki caught gazelles, wild pigs, and porcupines in his net. He was very pleased with himself. He made more nets; and each was a little better than the last.

One day Salifu said, "Wikki, why don't you go back to Spider and learn how to make better-shaped nets?"

So Wikki went again to the spider. "Please, Spider," he said, "will you show me how to shape a net?"

The spider showed him how to weave between the sticks of a bush.

Wikki made his nets on bushes for a long time. The nets were

21

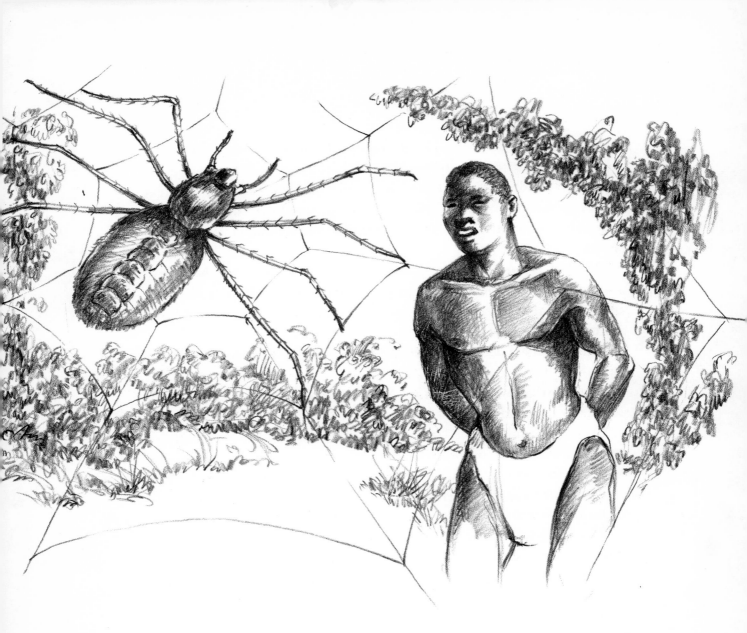

better-shaped than the first ones he had made. But it was hard to find good bushes for weaving.

One day Salifu said, "Why do you hunt for a bush every time you want to make a net? Can't you cut some long sticks and make a bush right here in the compound?"

22

Wikki set up some sticks in the clearing outside his hut. He soon learned that he needed only four of them. Nets made on four sticks were the best shape of all — square!

One day, as Salifu was watching him weave, she said, "Why do you make only big nets of rope? Why not make a small one of grass?"

Wikki did. But Salifu was still not satisfied. "Go back to Spider," she said, "and ask him to teach you now to make fine thread."

Wikki went to Spider. "Please, Spider," he said, "will you show me how to make thread?"

The spider showed him how the thread came out of his belly.

Wikki said, "You pass me, Spider! I can't do that!"

But Wikki found some wild cotton and he twisted the fibers into long threads. Then he wove the thread back and forth until he had made a long strip.

When Salifu felt of the soft thing Wikki had made, she wrapped it around herself. And she said, "Wikki, you have made cloth! Now we won't have to wear strips of bark anymore."

Soon, every man in the village had a loom in his compound and was weaving cloth for his women.

The skill of weaving passed from tribe to tribe until all the people of West Africa had learned to make cloth for themselves.

The Sloogeh Dog and the Stolen Aroma

There was once a greedy African who through shrewd and some-
times dishonest dealings had become very rich. He was so rich in ivory
that he had a fence of tusks all around his compound. He was so rich
in sheep that he dared not count them, lest the evil spirits become
jealous and destroy them.

He had so many wives that it took him from sunup to sundown just
to walk past the doors of their huts. And he had so many daughters
of marriageable age that he kept them in a herd guarded day and
night by old women.

The favorite pastime of this rich man was eating. But no guest ever
dipped the finger in the pot with him at mealtime. No pet sat near him
waiting to pick up fallen crumbs.

He ate alone in the shade of a big tree near the ivory gate of his
compound. He ate much food and he became very fat.

One day as he sat on his eating stool, a procession of wives filed over to him from the cookhouse. Each carried on her head a basket or platter or bowl of food.

Each put her offering before him and backed away to sit on her heels and watch him eat. This day among the delicacies were baked elephant's foot, fried locusts, and rice balls with peanut gravy.

A wonderful aroma came from the steaming food. It flooded the compound and seeped through and over the ivory fence.

Now it happened that, at the very moment the smell of the food was spreading through the jungle, the Sloogeh Dog was coming down a path near the rich man's gate. In his wanderings he had foolishly crossed the hot, barren "hungry country" and he was truly on the verge of starvation.

When the smell of the rich man's food met him, his head jerked up and saliva gathered at the corners of his mouth. New strength came into his long lean body. He trotted, following the scent, straight to the rich man's gate.

The Sloogeh Dog pushed on the gate. It was tied fast, so he peered between the ivory posts. Seeing the man eating meat off a big bone, he made polite little begging sounds deep in his throat.

Saliva made two long threads from the corners of his mouth to the ground.

The sight of the hungry creature at his very gate spoiled the rich man's enjoyment of his food. He threw a vex and bellowed, "Go away from my face, beggar!"

The Sloogeh Dog was outside the fence where anyone was free to be. He knew he didn't have to go away. But he had another idea. He trotted all the way around the compound searching for the pile of rich scraps which he was sure would be somewhere near the fence. He found not so much as a peanut shuck.

However, he didn't forget the wonderful smell of that food. Each day, at mealtime, he would come to sniff and drool at the rich man's gate. Each day the man would drive him away. And every day his anger grew until one day he left his food and went straight to the Council of Old Men.

He told his story. Then he said, "I want you to arrest that beggar of a dog!"

"On what grounds?" asked one of the old men.

"For stealing the aroma of my food!" said the rich man.

So the dog was arrested, a judge was appointed, and a day was set for the trial.

On the day of the trial, the whole village gathered about the Tree of Justice. From the start, the sympathy of the people was all with the Sloogeh Dog, for there was scarcely one of them who had not been swindled by the rich man.

But the judge was a just man. "I agree that the aroma was part of the food and so belonged to the accuser," he said. "And since the dog came every day to enjoy the smell of the food, one must conclude that it was intentional."

Murmurs of pity came from the crowd.

The Sloogeh Dog yawned nervously.

The judge continued. "If he had stolen only once, the usual punishment would be to cut off his paws!"

The Sloogeh Dog's legs gave way under him and he slithered on his belly to a hiding place back of the Tree of Justice.

"However," cried the judge, "since the crime was a daily habit, I must think about it overnight before I decide on a suitable punishment."

At sunup the next morning the people gathered to hear the sentence. They became very curious when the judge came leading a horse.

He dropped the reins to the ground and left the animal standing where the trail enters the village.

Was the horse part of the punishment? Was the judge taking a trip later? He only shrugged when the people questioned him.

The judge called the rich man and the Sloogeh Dog to come before him. Handing a kiboko to the rich man, he said, "The accused will be beaten to death by the accuser!"

The rich man took off his gold-embroidered robe. He made a practice swing through the air with the whip.

The judge held up his hand. "Wait!" he commanded.

Then he turned to the people. "Do the people agree that it was the invisible part of the food, and therefore its spirit, that was stolen?"

"Ee, ee!" cried the people.

The judge held up his hand again. "Do the people agree that the spirit of the dog is his shadow?"

"Ee, ee!" they said.

"Then," boomed the judge, "since the crime was against the spirit of the food, *only* the spirit of the dog shall be punished!"

The people howled with laughter. Their feet drummed on the hard-packed earth. They slapped each other's backs and shouted, "Esu! Esu!"

The Sloogeh Dog leaped up and licked the judge's nose.

The judge turned to the rich man and, when he could be heard, he said, "The shadow is big now, but you must beat it until the sun is straight up in the sky. When there is nothing left of the shadow, we shall agree that it is dead."

The rich man threw down the whip, picked up his garment, and said, "I withdraw the charges."

The judge shook his head. "You caused the arrest," he said. "You wanted the trial. Now administer justice. And if the kiboko touches so

30

much as a hair of the Sloogeh Dog, it will be turned upon you!"

There was nothing for the rich man to do but swing the whip hour after hour. The people watched and laughed as the dog leaped and howled, pretending to suffer with his shadow.

As the sun climbed higher and higher, the shadow became smaller and smaller — and much harder to hit. The whip became heavier in the man's flabby hands. He was dripping with sweat and covered with dust stirred up by the whip.

When the man could hardly bear the ordeal any longer, the dog lay down. That made it necessary for the man to get on his knees and put his arm between him and the dog to keep from touching a hair. When he brought down the whip, he hit his arm.

The people screamed with laughter.

The rich man bellowed and threw the kiboko. Then he leaped to the back of the judge's horse and rode headlong out of the village.

"He won't come back," said the oldest Old Man. "He would get *his* paws chopped off if he did. He stole the judge's horse!"

The Sloogeh Dog slunk off toward the rich man's house, his long nose sniffing for a whiff of something cooking beyond the ivory gate.

Madame Giraffe

In the Ondo bush three days' walk south of Timbuktu there is a water hole. The water there is so sweet and cool that animals came to it from far and near at drinking time.

One evening a gazelle, an elephant, and some monkeys were drinking and visiting when a giraffe came panting up. The animals were delighted to see Madame Giraffe, for she was seldom seen in that part of the forest.

Madame Giraffe spread her long front legs and arched her neck down to the water. When she had finished drinking she said, "I was grazing too far from my own drinking place. I thank you for sharing yours with me."

"You are very welcome," said Elephant. "We are always glad to see you, Madame Giraffe."

"Yes, you are most welcome," added Lion, who had come out of the bush just in time to hear the conversation.

A monkey who loved to tease Lion called down from a tree, "It's a shame that the king himself has come late to drink. But at least we had Elephant here to greet our guest."

32

Now, Elephant, who never could understand why the animals hadn't chosen him as their king, loved to tease Lion, too. "Perhaps our noble king has been visiting Leopard," he said.

The animals laughed. They knew that Lion hated Leopard because he wouldn't obey him.

33

Lion snarled. He wanted to bite Elephant, but he contented himself with saying, "You have a big head, Elephant, but that doesn't mean that you have a big brain."

Madame Giraffe doubled over with laughter. "That's true, Lion!" she cried. "Look at my little head. You can't judge a brain by the size of the head."

It pleased Lion that Madame Giraffe agreed with him. So, when she asked him to escort her back to her own country, he started off with her happily.

Elephant mumbled, "I would have taken Madame Giraffe home, if she had asked me."

The giraffe overheard and called back, "Perhaps some other time, Elephant."

Madame Giraffe led Lion along the trail by which she had come. When the two passed under a baobab tree, she sneezed. Then a leopard dropped out of the tree onto the lion's back.

There was a terrible fight, but at last the lion overcame the leopard and sat down to eat him.

Madame Giraffe, who had been watching from a little distance, came up and said, "You're a true hero! You saved my life, and I shall be grateful to you forever. I knew you would be a good protector."

"I saved your life so that I could eat you myself," said Lion. And he lunged at Madame Giraffe.

"Wait!" cried Madame Giraffe. "Don't eat me! Let me fetch that nice fat gazelle we saw at the water hole. She will be more tasty than I."

"Hurry then!" said Lion. To himself he added, "After she brings the gazelle, I'll head her off farther down the trail and eat her, too."

"Climb up that baobab tree and hide in the vines," said Madame

Giraffe. "I'll bring the gazelle down this same path. As we pass under the tree, I'll cough and you'll know it's time to spring."

Lion climbed the tree and the giraffe hurried back to the water hole. The animals were still there. Madame Giraffe said to Elephant, "I promised that you could escort me some other time. I didn't think it would be this soon."

Elephant was delighted to protect anyone so beautiful, and glad to prove he was more useful than Lion. He followed along close behind Madame Giraffe.

"Did our king fail you?" asked Elephant.

"You can't trust him!" said Madame Giraffe. "I learned that!"

"I wonder how long he will keep his throne by his good looks alone," said Elephant.

Presently Madame Giraffe stopped. "I have something to tell you before we go any farther," she said. "Remember when I came to the water hole the first time?"

Elephant nodded.

"On my way to the water," Madame Giraffe said, "a leopard dropped onto my back from a baobab tree. He would have eaten me if I had not promised to go to the water hole and fetch him a fat gazelle."

"You didn't get a gazelle," said Elephant.

"No," said Madame Giraffe. "I fetched a lion instead. And the lion killed the leopard. Now that stupid lion is letting me trick him the same way!"

"So!" cried Elephant, stopping in his tracks. "You're leading me into a trap! Do you think I'm going to let a lion pounce on my back? No thank you! Take yourself home!"

"Wait!" cried Madame Giraffe. "I have a plan. Lion is going to spring when I cough. Now, when we come to the baobab tree, I'll

yawn. That will be your sign to stop. Then, I'll cough and the lion will spring. He'll land on the ground in front of you and you can trample him!"

"But what if he sees me?" cried Elephant.

"The vines are very thick," said Madame Giraffe. "The leopard didn't see the lion. I'm sure he thought he was springing on a gazelle. Lion will think the same. Besides, if you kill Lion you will surely be made king in his place!"

"I *don't* like it!" said Elephant. But he didn't want Madame Giraffe to think him a coward so he followed on down the path.

Soon the two reached the baobab tree.

Madame Giraffe yawned.

Elephant stopped.

And Lion, who had forgotten the exact sign, sprang!

Madame Giraffe opened her mouth to cough, but she howled instead. Lion had landed right in the middle of her back! If it had not been for Elephant, she would have been killed.

"Lie down!" cried Elephant.

Madame Giraffe rolled outo her side. Then Elephant trampled Lion while he was still clinging to her back.

Madame Giraffe came out of the struggle with an ugly wound on her shoulder, but she lived. And since that day, to a giraffe the elephant is the king of the animal world.

Monkeys in the Sausage Tree

Long ago in a forest which bordered a veld in South Africa, there lived a colony of monkeys. They swarmed among the tangled vines and branches of the treetops. They ate wild plums, nuts, and bananas. And they were happy.

But there came a day when a tribe of Zulus built a village near the edge of that forest. The men picked the fruits which the monkeys thought belonged to them. And they hunted in the forest with spears.

From the time of the coming of men, the monkeys lived in fear. Twice they banded together and attacked the village. Each time the men heard their excited chatter while they were still a long way off, and they prepared an ambush.

As the monkeys approached, plumed and painted warriors sprang up out of the elephant grass and showered them with spears. Both times their chief had been the first to fall; and the others had fled, for monkeys will not fight without a chief.

Then a new chief was chosen — a new chief with a new plan. "We must take the men one at a time," he said. "We must hide in the trees along the paths and catch any man who walks alone. I will give one of my wives to anyone who helps to catch a man."

One day three young monkeys went out to hunt men. They found a sausage tree beside a path near the village. Each picked a hard, club-

shaped fruit of the tree and sat on a low branch to wait for a man to pass.

But no man came for what seemed a very long time.

Finally the three monkeys put aside their clubs and began to play. They chased each other round and round and up and down the sausage tree. They swung from hand to hand. They hung by their feet. They hung by two hands, one hand, and no hands — as they let themselves fall to lower branches.

But suddenly one of them began to scream. His tail was caught in a crotch of the tree. He pulled and pulled. His friends pried and pulled, but they couldn't get the tail loose.

"We will have to cut it off," said the oldest of the three.

"Cut it off!" cried the owner of the tail. "I will never let you do that! With no tail I would look like a man. Even my mother would drive me away."

The others knew that was true, and they began to pull and pry again. While they were struggling to free their friend, they heard the footsteps of a man coming along the path.

Picking up their clubs, the two free monkeys crouched, ready to attack.

But the monkey whose tail was caught said, "If we speak kindly to the man, maybe he can help me. When I am free I will help you catch him."

The other two agreed and they hid their clubs.

As the man drew near, the monkey who was trapped called out, "Please, Man, will you help me free my tail? It has been caught in the crotch of these branches for days. And I am about to die of hunger."

The man looked up and saw that the monkey's tail really was caught. But he also saw the two friends of the monkey sitting near. "Why don't your brothers help you?" he asked.

"We've tried," said one of them. "We have been trying for weeks."

The monkey whose tail was caught said, "I've heard that men are wise past all monkeys. If you can tell me how to escape, I will — "

"You will attack me!" said the man.

"Oh, never!" said the monkey. "We wouldn't do that!"

One of the other monkeys said, "Tell us how to free our friend and we shall be your friends forever."

"If it's advice you want," said the man, coming closer to see better, "I think I know what to do. You see those two big branches that come together to make the crotch that holds the tail? One of you stand on one branch, and the other on the other branch."

The two monkeys scrambled to the two branches that made the fork.

"When I say 'jump,'" said the man, "you jump up and come down hard. Ready? Jump!"

The monkeys jumped. The branches creaked. And out popped the tail.

The monkeys thanked the man and called to him, "Go softly," as he hurried on his way.

But after they had let him go, they were sorry that they had been so softhearted. "We were foolish," said the oldest monkey. "He helped us, but he is still our enemy!"

The others agreed. And soon they were swinging swiftly through the trees after the man. They overtook him just outside the village gate. They caught him with their powerful arms and began to drag him off.

"So this is the way you repay me for my kindness," said the man.

"We meant to let you go," said the monkey whose tail had been caught. "But our chief has promised to give a reward for every man caught. And we want to be the first to claim it."

42

Now the man knew that monkeys hate men first and snakes second. "Would your chief reward you if you brought in a snake, also?" he asked.

The monkeys talked together. If a man could be exchanged for a wife, perhaps a snake would be worth at least a bunch of bananas, they decided.

The man saw that they were considering the matter. "I have set a trap for a snake," he said. "If you will take me to it, you might have a snake to bring to your chief, also. And before I die, I would like to know if my trap has worked."

The monkeys had never seen a snake trap and they were curious. They agreed to go to the trap.

The trap was not a snake trap at all. It was a net to catch wart hogs. The clever man led the monkeys straight into it. Then he pulled a rope and had them all trapped inside together.

"Next time perhaps you'll remember not to reward a good deed with an evil one," said the man. But he knew — and the monkeys knew — there wouldn't be any next time for them.

"Monkeys in the Sausage Tree" is a folk tale from the Sudan. But the author has taken the liberty of giving it a South African setting. The sausage tree grows in both places.

The sausage tree usually grows to a height of about 30 feet, with a trunk two to three feet in diameter. It has large leathery leaves; and its dark red flowers and sausage-shaped fruit hang from long stems. The sausages are woody, hard, and heavy and are not good to eat. The botanical name is *kigelia pinnata*.

There are a few sausage trees in Florida, but they were imported from Africa.

43

Nansii and the Eagle

It was the "hungry time," the dry season, in Liberia. The forest folk were close to starvation, and Nansii, Father Spider, was hungriest of all.

One day he said to Hare, "I am starving for meat. Let's go hunting and see what luck we have."

"I'll go," said Hare, "if you'll promise to share whatever we shoot." Hare knew Nansii too well to trust him.

"Of course we'll share," said Nansii.

The two hurried to their homes for their bows and arrows. They met again on the path and set out. They hadn't gone far when they found a palm nut tree with a few nuts left on it. They were sitting under the tree eating the nuts when an eagle alighted on a bombax tree nearby.

Hare leaped up and shot the big bird. It came down with a great flutter.

"Look, look!" cried Hare. "We'll have meat for a week!"

"Meat for a week!" cried Nansii. "How can you say that? You've killed the Chief of Birds! You're in trouble. We'd better bury him quickly and tell no one. You don't want to go to jail, do you?"

"Jail!" gasped Hare with quivering whiskers. "You think they might put us in jail?"

"*You*, not me!" said Nansii. "Don't include me. I didn't shoot him. But I will help you bury him."

Hare started digging at once. He worked so hard that he didn't even notice that Nansii was scarcely helping at all.

"Let's leave one foot out," said Nansii.

Hare couldn't think of any good reason for not leaving one foot out. So that's what they did.

Then Hare set out for his farm, and Nansii for his. But Hare didn't go far. He hid behind a tree to watch. He had a feeling that Nansii might be up to some trick.

Soon he saw Nansii slipping back to the grave and pulling on the eagle's foot.

Hare called, "What are you doing, Nansii?"

"There are ants on the foot," said Nansii. "I'm getting them off."

Hare hurried over. There were ants on the foot, and Nansii was getting them off. There was nothing wrong with that as far as he could see.

The two parted again and went to their homes. But Nansii didn't stay there long. When he felt sure that Hare would no longer be spying around the eagle's grave, he went back and pulled it up by the foot.

Nansii dragged the bird home and told his wife, Zialee, to cook it for him. Then he said, "I'm going out to play in the clearing. When the soup is done I don't want you calling out, 'The eagle soup is ready.' I'll tie this rope to my leg and when the soup is done, you pull the rope and say nothing."

45

Nansii tied one end of a long rope to his leg and gave the other end to Zialee. Then he went out.

He was so happy about the big meal he would soon be eating that he made up a song which he sang over and over as he danced about in the dry grass. He sang:

"Something cooks in Nansii's house;
Let no one pass behind me.
Soup for a chief and a chief in the soup;
Let no one pass behind me.
Hare shoots the meat for Spider to eat.
Let no one pass behind me."

Now, it happened that Hare had decided to spend the evening at Nansii's house. As he was coming down the path, he heard Nansii singing and saw him dancing in the clearing. But Nansii sang softly and the only words Hare could make out were, "Let no one pass behind me."

"Now that's curious," said Hare to himself. Instead of greeting Nansii openly, he circled around to see what was behind him. He found the rope, with one end tied to Nansii's leg and the other end trailing all the way to his house.

Hare cut the rope in the middle and tied one end to his own leg. He left the loose piece still dragging behind the spider. Then he sat down to wait.

Hare waited and waited. The sun went down and it grew very dark in the forest. Then the rope jerked and Zialee, saying nothing as Nansii had commanded, pulled Hare into the hut.

There sat a great pot full of eagle soup. Hare ate every bit of it as fast as he could. Then setting the empty pot down, he hurried away without so much as saying "thank you" to Zialee.

Nansii finally became tired of waiting for Zialee to pull the rope. He decided to go and see why the soup was taking so long.

He went to his house and, finding the pot empty, he cried, "Zialee, where's my soup?"

Zialee came out of the corner where she had been resting. "Your soup! You ate it. I pulled the rope and you came in and ate it."

"You pulled the rope!" screeched Nansii. "I waited and waited and never felt one little tug. And I *know* I didn't eat the soup!"

Zialee looked into the kettle. "It's gone," she said. "If you didn't eat it, who did?"

"You did!" cried Nansii, and he began to beat her.

Hare heard Zialee's screams and he bounded back to Nansii's hut and put his head in the door.

"Why are you beating your wife?" he demanded.

"She ate my soup and then lied about it," said Nansii.

"What kind of soup?" asked Hare.

Nansii couldn't tell Hare it was eagle soup, so he said, "Crab soup."

"For shame!" cried Hare. "Fighting over crab soup!"

"He's lying," said Zialee. "It was eagle soup from the eagle you shot."

Nansii scurried up the wall and tried to hide himself in the thatch of the roof. But the rope was still tied to his leg; and it dangled straight down from the pole behind which he was hiding.

Hare reached for the rope. But Nansii was quicker. Twice around the pole he ran. Then the wood held the rope and Hare could not pull it down.

"You'll have to climb up to get me," taunted Nansii.

Hare tried to climb the rope, but he had never done that before and he kept slipping.

47

Zialee said, "I'll show you how! Let me go first and you follow. Do just as I do!"

While Zialee and Hare climbed the rope, Nansii worked at the knot which held it to his leg. The two had almost reached the top, when the knot loosened! Then, twice back around the pole Nansii scurried with the end of the rope.

And poof! Hare landed on the dried mud floor with a tangle of rope and Zialee on top.

Hare brushed himself off and shook a paw at Nansii. Then to Zialee he said, "If he tries to beat you again, tell him it was I who ate the soup. And it served him right!"

Zialee began to giggle. She pointed to Hare's hind leg.

The other piece of rope was still tied to it.

How Dog Outwitted Leopard

In the early days in Uganda, Dog and Leopard were friends. They lived together in a cave, sharing the work and sharing their food.

But Leopard was stronger and bolder than Dog, and a better hunter. Before long Dog began to grow fat on the game brought in by his partner. The fatter he grew, the lazier he became, until he stopped hunting altogether.

At first Dog tried to cover up his failure to bring home meat. He invented stories about wart hogs or rabbits which he had *almost* caught. After a time he decided he must think of a better way of deceiving his friend.

And he did.

One evening Leopard said, "I've been watching a black goat down in the village of people. I think it is fat enough for eating, and tonight I'm going to get it."

"Did you say a *black* goat?" asked Dog. "That's odd. I've had my eye on a black goat, too. I think I shall go hunting myself tonight."

The two friends slept until the darkest hour just before the dawn. Then they loped off to the village. They parted near the village fence, Dog going one way and Leopard the other.

Dog ran a little way, then retraced his steps and followed Leopard from a little distance.

Leopard picked his way along the fence until he came to a goat pen. Then he backed away, gave a run, and easily cleared the palings. He killed the black goat, flung it over his shoulder, and leaped back over the fence.

At that moment Dog beat the ground and the fence with a big stick. He changed his voice and shouted, "Leopard has stolen a goat! Catch him! Catch him! There he goes! Give me that spear!"

Leopard thought the whole village was after him. He dropped the goat and ran for his life.

Then Dog trotted over, picked up the goat, and dragged it home to the cave.

"Come and see my goat!" he called to Leopard. "Isn't it a fat one! Where's your goat?"

Leopard told him of his bad luck.

"What a shame!" said Dog. "You and I will share this one."

Leopard helped build a fire to cook the goat.

When the meat was almost ready, Dog slipped out of the cave. He ran to a place just out of sight of the entrance and began beating the ground with a stick. "Ou! Ou!" he shouted. "Don't kill me! It was Leopard who killed your goat! Ou! Ou! Ou!"

Back in the cave Leopard said to himself, "The men have tracked me to my den. They are killing Dog and they will kill me next." And off he streaked into the forest.

When Dog saw that his trick had worked, he went back into the cave and ate the goat all by himself.

At dusk Leopard returned and saw Dog lying all stretched out, too full of meat to move.

Dog moaned, "Don't touch me, my friend. Those men nearly killed me! In fact they left me for dead!"

"Poor fellow!" said Leopard. "Just lie there and rest. Nothing heals like a good rest. I'll fetch us another goat soon."

Two nights later, Leopard went hunting again. Dog sneaked after him and tricked him as before, bringing in the goat himself, and then eating it himself.

Leopard was very much embarrassed by his failures. He still hadn't caught on to Dog's treachery. He decided to seek help from Muzimu, the spirit of the forest.

He found Muzimu deep in the heart of the jungle where vines coil around the trees and hang in long loops over a little black pool.

Leopard called into the pool. "Oh, Muzimu, have pity on me! Once I was a matchless hunter. Now I am dying of hunger. Though I still catch my prey, I am always driven away from it. Tell me, Muzimu, how my good luck may return."

Leopard listened. From deep down in the pool came a faint voice.

51

"Watch Dog. You know how to catch prey. Dog knows how to eat it. Watch Dog!"

Leopard couldn't understand how watching his friend would make his good luck return, but he decided to follow the advice.

The next night Leopard said, "I have spotted a tan goat that looks good to me. I am going to try to get it and *keep* it, this time."

"A *tan* goat?" said Dog. "I know where there are some tan goats, too. I think I'll go hunting with you tonight."

The two traveled together to the edge of the village, then separated just as before.

Leopard leaped over the fence near the goat pen, killed a tan goat, and leaped back over the palings with it.

Dog, who was hiding nearby, began threshing about, beating the fence and calling out in a strange voice. "Leopard has stolen a goat! Kill him!"

This time Leopard did not run away. He ran toward the commotion. Then he saw Dog's ears sticking up above the tall grass.

Suddenly Leopard knew who had been frightening him! With a snarl he lunged after Dog.

Round and round the village, Dog ran for his life. At last he found an opening under the fence and squeezed through just in time.

In his terror he streaked across a garden and straight into the hut of a man.

The man leaped out of bed, caught up his spear, and was about to kill Dog. But that clever creature crouched low with his head between his forepaws and his tail wagging furiously. He cocked his head and looked into Man's face. He whimpered softly, and Man understood that all he wanted was to be his friend.

And to this day, Man and Dog are fast friends, but Leopard and Dog are sworn enemies.

52

Koi and the Kola Nuts

One day in a village of West Africa the chief died. So the wisest old man of the tribe was called to divide the chief's possessions among the sons.

The wise man counted out to each of them so many cows, so many sheep, and so many tusks of ivory. He had just finished when along came Koi, the youngest son. Koi had been hunting and no one had bothered to call him.

There was not so much as a lamb left for him.

The wise man was wisest in ways of avoiding work. He did not bother to redivide the possessions. He looked around until he found a scraggly little kola tree. He gave that to Koi as his inheritance.

"You've cheated me!" cried Koi. "I'll go to a land where the people will treat me as the son of a chief!"

So Koi ran away, but first he picked all the kola nuts from his little tree. He wrapped them in a mat, tied them on a kinja, and swung the load onto his back.

54

Koi traveled for many days. At last he came to a mountain. He struggled up it with his load of kola nuts, and then started down the other side.

As he was climbing down the mountain he met a snake. The snake was hurrying along, looking this way and that, as though he were hunting for something he couldn't find.

"What is the matter, Friend Snake?" asked Koi.

"My mother is ill," said the snake, "and she must have kola medicine or she will die."

"Look no farther," said Koi as he took down his kinja and dug out a few nuts.

"Thank you kindly," said the snake. "I hope I can do something for you someday."

Koi went on, pleased with himself for having made the snake happy. After a while he met an army of ants marching in an endless column about as wide as a kola nut.

Koi stepped aside to let the ants pass. As he did so, one of them called out to him in a thin voice, "Do you know where we could find a kola tree? By mistake we ate all the nuts in the forest devil's basket. He said we must replace them or — "

Koi never learned what the forest devil had said he would do. He already had the nuts unwrapped, and the ant was so happy to see them he didn't finish the sentence.

"How many do you need?" asked Koi.

"As many as the forest devil's fingers and toes," said the ant. He counted his own feet. "Six," he decided.

"The forest devil is a person," said Koi. "You will need twenty."

The ants took the nuts and marched back the way they had come.

As Koi neared the foot of the mountain, he met an alligator. The

55

great beast was crying and dragging himself along as though he would never reach his destination.

"What is your trouble?" asked Koi.

"I ate the rain maker's dog," said the alligator. "If I had known whose dog it was, I wouldn't have eaten it."

"What difference does that make?" asked Koi. "It's as bad to eat one dog as another!"

"Difference!" cried the alligator. "The rain maker is going to strike me dead with a lightning bolt if I don't pay him a kinjaful of kola nuts by tomorrow! There aren't that many kola nuts on this side of the mountain."

"How do you know there aren't?" said Koi as he crawled out from under his load. He unwrapped a corner of the mat.

The alligator smiled a big toothy smile.

"If I give them to you I won't have to carry them any more," said Koi. And he fastened the kinja to the alligator's broad back.

By evening of the same day, Koi approached a village. The guard at the gate stopped him. "Who comes to the village of the Great Chief Fulikolli?" he asked.

Koi stood proudly. "I am Koi, from the land beyond the mountain," he said. "I am the son of a chief."

Now, Koi was covered with dust from the trail, and his arms and legs were scratched from the rocks on the mountain. The guard looked at him and said, "You talk big for a beggar!"

"I have run away from home," said Koi. "May I be a guest at your village?"

A crowd of village people began to gather around the guard.

"A beggar! A beggar!" cried a wicked-looking old woman. "Put him in the cooking pot!"

Then Chief Fulikolli came out. "What have we here?" he asked.

Koi stood before him. "I am Koi," he said, "the son of a chief from over the mountain. Will you please allow me to be your guest?"

"He's a beggar! He's a beggar!" the people shouted. "Let's eat him!"

"Wait!" said the chief. "We shall try him. If he can chop down that palm tree so that it falls toward the forest instead of toward the village we will let him go. If the tree falls toward the village we will eat him."

The people laughed!

Koi trembled when he saw the tree. It leaned toward the village so sharply that it looked as though a small wind could topple it.

"Please," Koi begged the chief, "will you send the people away and let me cut down the tree after dark?"

The chief agreed.

An ax was given to Koi. He sat with it under the tree and waited

57

for darkness to come. As he waited he wept. How could the tree be made to fall toward the forest?

Suddenly he heard a shuffling noise nearby. There was the snake whom he had helped earlier that day. "I've tracked you a long way," said the snake. "I want to tell you that the kola medicine cured my mother and she sends her thanks."

"That's kind of your mother," said Koi. "But nothing can comfort me now. I must chop down this palm so that it falls toward the forest, or tomorrow I die!"

"But it leans the wrong way," said the snake.

"Exactly!" said Koi. "It's a trick. The people of this village are making sport of me before they eat me."

"I'll get my great-uncles, the pythons," said the snake. "Maybe they can help."

At moonrise the snake returned with three huge pythons. The great snakes wrapped their tails around the crooked palm tree and their necks around a nearby bombax tree.

Then Koi chopped with all his might. When the last fiber of the palm trunk was cut, the snakes pulled the tree over so that it fell toward the forest.

When Chief Fulikolli saw the fallen tree the next morning, he said, "Look, the boy has felled the tree toward the forest. He shall go free!"

But the people were not to be deprived of a feast so easily. "Put him in the pot! Put him in the pot!" they shouted.

"Let us test him one more time," said the chief. "We will scatter ten baskets of rice all over my fields. If he can pick up every grain in the dark of the night we shall let him go. If he fails, we shall eat him."

As soon as darkness came, Koi went out with a basket. He began to feel about on the ground for grains of rice. He scarcely found any at all! Tears fell from his eyes as he bent over the ground.

A tear happened to fall on the head of an ant. "Rain!" cried the ant. Then he saw Koi. "Why, it isn't rain," the ant said. "It's a boy, crying! Aren't you the boy who gave us kola nuts two days ago?"

"Yes," said Koi. "And now I'm in trouble. I must pick up ten baskets of rice before morning or I'll be eaten!"

"You fetch the baskets, and my people will pick up the rice," said the ant.

Soon the farm was crawling with ants, and every one of them was picking up rice as fast as he could.

In the morning the ten baskets of rice stood before the house of the chief. When Chief Fulikolli saw the rice and Koi standing proudly beside it, he said, "You have done well! You shall go free."

But the people gathered around. "It's a trick," said one.

"He couldn't have done it," said another.

Then Koi heard one whisper, "Let the chief free him. We'll catch him before he goes very far."

Koi said to the chief, "The people are planning to overtake me. I'm afraid to go!"

Chief Fulikolli stood before the people and spoke in a big voice. "Let us test this boy one more time. I shall throw my medicine ring into the deepest part of the river. If he can bring it back, will you honor him as the son of a chief?"

The people loved tests of any kind. "We promise," they shouted.

The chief spoke again. "If he brings back the ring, I shall give him half of this village and my loveliest daughter for a wife."

All the people of the village went to the river to watch the chief throw his ring in. Then they left Koi alone at the waterside.

Koi looked at the deep dark water of the river. "Even the chief is trying to destroy me," he said. "I cannot even swim!"

Just then he saw the mud-gray nose of an alligator streaking toward him from downriver.

The alligator grinned when he saw Koi. "Do you remember me?" he called.

"I am not sure," said Koi, for all alligators looked alike to him.

"You gave me your kola nuts," said the alligator, "and they saved me from the rain maker!"

"Good!" said Koi. "But you are seeing me for the last time. I must bring Chief Fulikolli's medicine ring up from the bottom of the river by sunup tomorrow, or I shall be eaten!"

"Perhaps I can help you," said the alligator. He dived under the water and came up with a small clamshell. He dived again and brought up a sea worm. In and out of the water he went all night. Just as the sun was rising, he came up proudly waving the ring at the end of a claw!

When the chief saw that Koi had recovered the ring from the river, he put a striped robe on him. In the presence of all the people he said, "Half of the village north of a line drawn east from the fallen palm tree, I give to Chief Koi!"

Then out from a nearby hut came the most beautiful girl Koi had ever seen. "This is my daughter," said the chief. "She shall be your wife."

"A wedding! A wedding!" cried the people. " Now we shall have a feast after all!"

The Prince Who Wanted the Moon

Where the Aruwimi River flows into the Congo there once lived a people called the Bandimba. They were ruled by a rich and powerful king named Bahanga.

King Bahanga had many wives and hordes of children. But his children were all girls. He had no son to inherit the kingdom. His subjects seemed to have more sons than daughters, and he envied the poorest among them.

At last King Bahanga married a daughter of his favorite chief. She bore him a son.

The king was so happy to have a son that he granted the boy's every wish. He even shared his power with the little prince, making him ruler of all the children. Since the children were more numerous than their parents, it turned out that the boy ruled more subjects than his father.

Many possessions and much power only made the boy unhappy. The more he had, the more he wanted. Every day he came to his father with some new request.

One day the prince was playing with the boys of his court. When he grew tired he lay down in a hammock to rest. The boys sat in a circle at a respectful distance.

Afer a time, the prince leaped to his feet and cried out, "There is no one in the world as rich as I. My father withholds nothing from me. I ask and I get what I want!"

Then the puniest of the boys said in a timid voice, "I know one thing your father can't give you."

"What?" asked the prince.

"The moon," said the boy. And the other boys doubled over with laughter.

The prince went to his father and told him that the boys were taunting him because he did not have the moon among his toys.

"The moon!" cried the king. "The moon is a long way up. How should we ever be able to reach it?"

"But father," whined the prince, "I must have it. How can I face my friends? If you don't get it for me I shall die!"

"Rest your mind," said the king. "I shall call all the wise men of the kingdom together. If they say the moon can be brought down, you shall have it."

The state drum was rolled out and a message was drummed to every village in the kingdom, calling the wise men to a great palaver.

When all were assembled, the king asked the wise men whether or not the moon could be reached and brought down to earth.

Now, no one in Bandimba Land had ever heard of anyone's going higher than the treetops, so all the wise men were bewildered. They looked from one to another, afraid to speak.

At last the youngest of them rose and said, "Long life to King Bahanga! I, his slave, am able to reach the moon, if the king's power will aid me."

The boldness of the young wise man made the others feel ashamed and they turned to him, half-believing what he said.

"Speak on!" they said.

"If it please the king," said the young wise man, "I shall go up to the moon from the top of the mountain near the Cataract of Panga. I shall build a scaffold, and on it one-more-again, and on *it* one-more-again, and so on until I reach the moon."

"But is it possible to reach the moon that way?" asked the king.

"Of course!" said the young wise man. "If we build high enough! It will take an army of workmen. If the king commands it, it shall be done."

64

"Be it so," said the king. "I place every man in the kingdom at your service."

"The men are not enough," said the young wise man. "It will take every woman in the land to cook and feed the workmen. We shall need every boy to carry water and to strip the bark off vines for binding the timbers. We shall need every girl to plant gardens and raise cassava for food."

Thus it was that all the people in the kingdom were put to work to bring down the moon for a toy for the little prince.

In a few days the scaffolds stood as tall as the tallest trees. In a few weeks the structure had grown to several arrow flights. When the edge of the year came around, it was so high up in the sky that the top of it could no longer be seen.

The work went on and on. At last the young wise man sent word down that the tower would soon be finished. Everyone believed him, and people from far and near came to watch the plucking of the moon.

All but one old wise man. He loaded his family into a bongo and paddled up the Aruwimi River.

A week after the flight of the old wise man, the young wise man sent word for the king to come up the tower. The prince wanted to go with him.

So it was that as the moon came up that night, the king, the prince, and the young wise man waited for it at the very top of the tower.

As the moon came close, the king reached out and touched it. "It is hot!" he cried. "It is too hot to play with!"

The prince jumped up and down so that the tower swayed. "I want it! I want it!" he screamed.

"I'll have to throw a rope around it," said the young wise man. And he did. Then he pulled and pulled, but the moon was firmly fixed. The king and the prince caught hold of the rope and pulled, too.

Then there was a great sound.

The moon burst open!

Hot melted rock poured down over the king and the prince and all the workmen on the tower. The wood of the structure caught fire and it became a flaming torch.

The molten rock kept pouring out of the moon until it flooded down the mountain and streamed over the plain.

All the people in the country would have been killed if a wonderful thing had not happened. The big people suddenly turned into gorillas and baboons, and the children turned into all sorts of long-tailed monkeys.

As monkeys they swung easily through the treetops and escaped. Their descendants inhabit the jungle trees of all Africa to this day.

NOTES ON THE STORIES

"Tricksy Rabbit" is a very old story. A man of the Waganda tribe, named Sabadu, told it to the famous explorer Henry M. Stanley about 80 years ago. He said it was told to him when he was a little boy.

Sabadu gave a high-pitched voice to the rabbit, a deep bass voice to the elephant, a mooing tone to the buffalo; and when he yapped, he sounded exactly like a dog. He was a good storyteller.

"Wikki, the Weaver" is an original story. It may have some foundation in fact. The true name of the inventor of the cloth loom in Africa has been lost. Wikki is a name taken from the Fan tribe in West Africa.

"The Sloogeh Dog and the Stolen Aroma" was collected by Louise Stinetorf in the Belgian Congo, but it is believed to have originated in North Africa. The Sloogeh Dog is a folk-tale character familiar to African children just as Br'er Rabbit is familiar to American youngsters.

The word *sloogeh* is probably a corruption of the word *saluki,* which is the name of the greyhound-like animal once used as a racing dog by Egyptian kings.

"Madame Giraffe" is a story supposedly told by Kplowo, a boy guide, to Bata Kindai Amgoza Ibn LoBagola as the two lay in the matted vines of a tree along the trail near the borders of Egba. It was told as a going-to-sleep story to help them forget the dangers of the trail.

"Monkeys in the Sausage Tree" is a folk tale of the Sudan country. It is meant to teach a lesson.

The sausage tree grows to a height of about 30 feet, with a trunk about three feet in diameter. It has large leathery leaves, dark red flowers, and sausage-shaped fruit about two feet long and two or three inches thick. The sausages are woody, hard and heavy, and not good to eat. The botanical name is *kigelia pinnata.*

"Nansii and the Eagle" is a folk tale of the Kpelli tribe in Liberia. Miss Carolyn Hovingh, medical missionary to these people, says they love to tell stories around their cooking fires in their huts in the evenings.

67

Spider stories are especially popular in this area. When a child cries out in fear upon seeing a spider, his Ma will say, "Don't be afraid — that is only Nan Sii (or father spider, since *nan* means father and *sii,* spider)."

"How Dog Outwitted Leopard" is one of several versions of the story. Sarboko, who once was a page to the King of Uganda, claimed this to be the true one. The story is popular among all the tribes of the Nile River lake region.

"Koi and the Kola Nuts" is based upon a folk story which was put into writing in a little booklet used in the Each One Teach One campaign to teach adults in Liberia to read. The story is also read by children in the schools there.

Kola nuts grow wild in West Africa. Each seed pod contains several red and white nuts which are shaped something like horse chestnuts. They are chewed by the natives for their flavor as well as to prevent fatigue. They are used in medicine and in the popular kola-flavored soft drinks.

"The Prince Who Wanted the Moon" is a story collected by Henry M. Stanley in the late 1800's. On his journey up the Congo River, Mr. Stanley would gather his guides around a campfire in the evenings and offer pieces of cloth to anyone who would tell a story good enough to put into his book.

The storytellers were usually modest and would begin by saying they couldn't remember anything that was ever told them — then they would launch out on long, long tales.

BIBLIOGRAPHY

"Tricksy Rabbit" is adapted from a story entitled "The Partnership of Rabbit and Elephant and What Came of It" from Henry M. Stanley's *My Dark Companions and Their Strange Stories*, Charles Scribner's Sons, and the Press of J. J. Little, 1893.

"Wikki, the Weaver" is based on a story entitled "The Invention of the Cloth Loom," page 734 in *Travels in West Africa*, by Mary H. Kingsley, MacMillan and Company, New York, 1897.

"Nansii and the Eagle" is adapted from a translation of the story "Father Spider and the Eagle" from a pamphlet put out by the Literacy Center of Monrovia, Liberia, under the title "Liberian Fables Book I," March, 1954.

"Koi and the Kola Nuts" is based upon the story "Koi and His Heritage" found in a booklet entitled "Nemo and Other Stories" published by the National Fundamental Education Centre, Klay, Liberia, September, 1954.

"How Dog Outwitted Leopard" is condensed from a story by that name in Henry M. Stanley's *My Dark Companions and Their Strange Stories*, Charles Scribner's Sons, and the Press of J. J. Little Company, 1893.

"Monkeys in the Sausage Tree" is derived from the story "The Proper Reward for Treachery — The Monkeys and the Hunter," page 391 in the book *An African Savage's Own Story* by Bata Kindai Amgoza Ibn LoBagola. Copyright 1930 by Alfred A. Knopf, Inc., fifth printing, 1933.

"Madame Giraffe" is adapted from a story entitled "The Lion and the Leopard," page 298 in *An African Savage's Own Story* by Bata Kindai Amgoza Ibn LoBagola. Copyright 1930 by Alfred A. Knopf, Inc., fifth printing, 1933.

"The Sloogeh Dog and the Stolen Aroma" is based on a folk story told by Louise Stinetorf beginning on page 214 in her novel *Beyond the Hungry Country*, J. B. Lippincott Company, 1954.

"The Prince Who Wanted the Moon" is based on a story called "The Boy and the Moon" recorded in Henry M. Stanley's *My Dark Companions and Their Strange Stories*, Charles Scribner's Sons and the Press of J. J. Little & Company, 1893.

GLOSSARY

Tricksy Rabbit
>WATUSI: The world's tallest people, the men being seven feet tall or over, and the women almost as tall
>BWANA: Master

Wikki, the Weaver
>JU-JU: Charm
>ARMLET: Arm band worn above the elbow
>BUSH ROPE: Long leafless vines used for tying bundles
>LOOM: Weaving frame
>COMPOUND: Enclosure containing all the huts and grounds of a family

The Sloogeh Dog and the Stolen Aroma
>SLOOGEH DOG: Saluki dog, the long-eared desert hound often teamed with falcons in hunting gazelles
>MARRIAGEABLE DAUGHTERS: A form of wealth in that each could be sold for a great price
>HUNGRY COUNTRY: Desert
>VEX: Fit of anger
>KIBOKO: Rhinoceros-hide whip
>EE (A): Yes
>ESU! (A-SU):Good! Wonderful!

Madame Giraffe
>BAOBAB: An African tree with a very thick trunk, few branches, and gourdlike fruit which is called "monkey bread"

70

Monkeys in the Sausage Tree

> VELD (FELDT): Field
>
> ZULUS: Tall, handsome negroes of South Africa who were once the fiercest enemies of the white settlers, but who now live quietly on their reservation
>
> GO SOFTLY: A farewell spoken to one person or a small party upon setting out on the trail — only a large well-armed company would dare to be noisy on the path

Nansii and the Eagle

> BOMBAX: A tall tree, also called silk cotton tree, which produces seed pods filled with kapok — used in the United States for upholstering furniture and filling life jackets
>
> JAIL: A pen, dungeon, or hut in which prisoners were kept — with no food provided except what was brought to them by friends

How Dog Outwitted Leopard

> WART HOGS: African wild pigs which have two pairs of tusks, and three pairs of "warts" between the eyes and upper tusks
>
> PALINGS: Long, pointed poles set close together to make a fence

Koi and the Kola Nuts

> KOLA NUTS: Nuts similar in shape to the horse chestnut which grow wild in West Africa; are used by the Africans as a medicine and stimulant, and are used to make kola-flavored drinks in the United States
>
> KINJA: A carrying frame made of sticks lashed together, worn on the back and held in place by straps about the shoulders and across the forehead

71

FOREST DEVIL: A tribesman who keeps his identity a secret and appears at ceremonies completely hidden by a raffia devil dress and wooden mask

RAIN MAKER: A wise man who supposedly has the power to bring rain or withhold it at will

PYTHONS: Snakes which, in Africa, grow to a length of about 20 feet, live in trees, and prey upon birds and small animals

The Prince Who Wanted the Moon

PALAVER: Conference

CASSAVA (KA-SAH-VAH): A small shrub whose roots are eaten like potatoes

ONE-MORE-AGAIN: Another

BONGO: Native dugout canoe